The Testicles of General Zia

The Testicles of General Zia

Frank Fuchs

Acocks Publisher

Birmingham

The Testicles of General Zia
ISBN: 978-1-9164116-0-9 (soft cover)
ISBN: 978-1-9164116-1-6 (e-book)

Contents

I am spared.
Buddha

'There should be no plural in the title of this book,'
a former Pakistani Prime Minister

Prologue

Another man, also naked from the waist upwards, materialized from somewhere. He carried a leather slap-paddle in his right hand.

The drumming stopped and the man with the slap-paddle bowed before the audience, turned towards one of the storytellers and asked, 'Your name?'

'Master Lither, sir,' the first storyteller replied, 'they call me Kameena.'

'Which son of a bitch named you *Kameena*?' Lither asked.

'Your father,' Kameena replied.

Kameena received a whack on his back from the slap-paddle.

The audience laughed. Kameena dodged another whack and Lither, waving his slap-paddle in the air, moved towards the second storyteller and asked him, 'And you are?'

'Kanjar, Master Lither.'

'And which bastard named you *Kanjar?*'

'You did.'

Lither struck him with his slap-paddle and asked both of them, 'And why are you here tonight?'

They chanted back in unison, 'To remember our departed leader, Mard-e-Momin-Mard-e-Haq, Zia ul Haq, Man of Purity-Man of Righteousness, Zia ul Haq,

'Let the competition begin,' Lither proclaimed loudly, 'This gori, this white woman, to the winner!'

Part I:
Kidnapped in
Pakistan

A stranger sent me a message that led to Iona Cumming, aka Tipsy, the woman I was trying to bed in Birmingham, going to Pakistan and getting kidnapped.

We both work at Acocks University in Birmingham, where I head the Academy of Subveritibable Syntaxes and Tipsy leads the Centre of Anti-androgynous Intersectional Genderisation of Disempowermental Discourses.

It was early March 2017 and I was in my office when an Akber Zeb Junior shared a video link, which he said was of a holy man in Pakistan. The video was dated 17th August 1987. It was of a bearded European man, perhaps in his late forties, with shoulder length curly brown hair, who kept repeating the same phrase in a very heavy Irish accent: *By the quivering cunt of the unfekked mother of Christ, fek Amereeka and fek General Zia with mangos.*

I wrote back to Akber Zeb Junior and asked him if this man was still alive. I also told him that in my opinion this was no holy man, and explained in plain English that 'fek' meant 'fuck', and that the speaker didn't think much of America or General Zia.

Akber Zeb Junior replied, saying that the man in the video used to be called Paddy Keir Hardie, but now went by the name of Pir Karmala Hardee, and that he could be found at Jabra Chouk in Islamabad.

Given Tipsy's obsession with trying to find her biological father, who she was convinced was Irish and had met her mother in Pakistan; I should have shared the post with Tipsy immediately, but didn't do so as I didn't want her to be disappointed again.

After concluding that there was no possibility of Tipsy working out where Jabra Chouk, the intersection of the Jaw, was in Islamabad, I decided to forward her the FB messages. She was in her office in the room next to mine at the time, and immediately telephoned me and said in an animated voice, 'Frank, why the hell did you send me this filth? It is just more of the misogynistic rubbish you claim to be subversive folk humour.'

She has not clocked the fact that the man in the video is Irish, I concluded, and that he is in Pakistan.

I replied to Tipsy, 'The value of this…'

'The only worth of *this* is that it gets you a big fat salary, and you are becoming more and more like the filth of your job!' Tipsy interrupted.

Perhaps this was true. I was indeed getting obsessed with sex, but her feminist outbursts against the central premise of my work, where I have collected thousands of subversive stories, or *dirty jokes* as Tipsy was fond of calling them, made me snap and I said, 'The problem with you left wing women is that you are so fucked up about the revolution, you forget you were made to fuck.'

'Oh god, you are impossible,' Tipsy said, slamming the phone down on me.

Keep your calm, Frank, I thought, don't say anymore. You are getting further away from her pants with each of your rants, but rang her back and said, 'And this *filth,* as you call it, robs the powerful of their moral authority.' I took a long breath and asked, 'And do you not think that the Catholic Church is slightly unhinged by phrases like the one I just sent you, or with the likes of *a priests balls are about as good as a nuns tits?*'

I took a breather while waiting for the predictable diatribe from Tipsy, and thought, you might as well wank about her now, Frank, you stupid twat.

Tipsy was silent and I asked, 'Well?'

'Sorry Frank,' she replied after a long pause, 'I went to the toilet, what did you say?'

Fuck you, I thought, but said, 'I was just saying that this subject needs to be discussed face to face in a calmer situation,' and ended the call.

Around an hour or so later, she telephoned me again and said, 'Don't leave before I see you today.'

I wasn't in the mood for any more arguments with her and replied, 'I need to have my cat neutered. I've booked the operation.' This was true. 'Can't stay late, sorry,' which was relatively true. I could stay if I thought she was going to drop her pants. The cat wouldn't mind waiting.

'Have you seen his face?' she asked, clearly not concerned about my cat.

'Whose?'

'The man in the FB link you forwarded me.'

'Yes,' I replied.

'It's not what he is saying,' she interjected, and then added, 'hang on,' before putting the phone down.

She burst into my room a few seconds later carrying a small folder with a number of photographs and a few notebooks. She spread some high definition printouts in front of me. These were enlarged pictures of the Irishman and a photograph of her mother.

Tipsy slid her mother's photograph towards me, saying, 'Was she gorgeous, or was she gorgeous?'

The resemblance with Tipsy was truly astounding. She was in her mid-30s, as old as Tipsy was now. They both had the same searching blue eyes and shoulder-length blond hair.

Though I looked at the printouts, in my mind I imagined seeing my wobbly pink arse as I fucked Tipsy.

'Well?' she asked.

'Well what?' I replied.

'Isn't there something rather striking about him?'

I focused on the image of the man again. He had a small pointed nose and eyes that seemed to be perfectly spaced. He was certainly a good looking man, I thought, but I just shrugged my shoulders.

'Look at his eyes,' Tipsy insisted.

I did.

I looked up at Tipsy. Her blond hair was raining down in waves. Her eyes were more beautiful than ever, set as they were under her perfectly trimmed brown eyebrows, which made her small nose look all the more perfect.

'And'?' she asked softly, as she ran her fingers through my hair and then perched her lovely arse on the edge of my desk.

Oh god, I thought, looking at her in her sleeveless black T-shirt, with her bulging cleavage and her short red skirt, which had made my dick throb.

She saw me looking at her exposed thighs and instead of her usual reprimand, smiled. A sensual sort of smile, and then she noticed the bulge in my trousers and protested, 'What's this, Frank?'

'It's not what you think,' I replied, putting my hand in front of my zip.

'Good,' she said and continued, 'She told me he was a British intelligence officer who had gone missing during a cross border incursion into Afghanistan with the Mujahideen.'

Tipsy placed a small notebook on the table, saying, 'This is Mother's notebook from 1982.' She opened a page, and there in clear handwriting was the first part of the phrase being repeated by the Irishman in the video: *By the quivering cunt of the unfekked mother of Jesus.*

'In the video, the man does not say *Jesus* but *Christ,*' I pointed out to Tipsy.

'Oh god, why are you always so pedantic?' Tipsy snapped back, '*Jesus, Christ,* it is all the same thing, for Christ's sake,' and added, 'it is not Mother's handwriting. It is definitely a man's. It could be my father's, Frank, it really could.'

'It doesn't prove that this man *is* your father, Tipsy.'

She nodded and placed another notebook in front of me, saying, 'Mother had been fascinated by Punjabi curses and swearing, and according to her notes, look at this.'

I nodded and read her mother's handwritten notes, entitled, **Punjabi curse from PKH**: *May your ears turn into arseholes and you shit all over your shoulders.*

'Why is *this* in your mother's notebook?' I asked, looking at the hand drawn heart next to the letters PKH.

'Maybe it was from another random man she picked up in Pakistan, or wherever she picked them up from,' Tipsy said bitterly.

'Don't be so harsh on your mum,' I said. 'She must have been a lovely woman to have raised someone as wonderful as you.'

'Oh, thanks,' Tipsy said softly.

Yes, Frank, I thought, change tact.

'Now play the video clip again,' Tipsy said.

I did.

When it ended, she asked, 'Has it hit you yet?' but before I could answer, she continued, 'When exactly did General Zia die?'

I shook my head and typed a query into Google. Google replied: *August 17, 1988.*

'Now go back to the video clip,' Tipsy said.

I did.

'Look at the date in the time code of the video,' Tipsy said. 'And you know there is a theory that General Zia's plane was blown up with a bomb smuggled on-board in a crate of mangoes.'

It said: 17th August 1987, exactly one full year before the actual incident.

'Now, do you still think it is just a rant of a drunken Pakistani Irishman?' Tipsy asked, beaming with the smile of a little girl who was about to meet her father.

'You are a genius,' I said in all honesty.

'Where is the Jabra Chouk in Islamabad,' she asked coyly.

I couldn't resist the innocence of her smile and told her.

A few days later, I received an email from Tipsy. She had gone to Pakistan to find her father, and forbade me to mention this to anyone lest news got out and he went into hiding.

I didn't see Tipsy again until I went out to search for her and ended up being kidnapped myself.

*****

It was a beautiful moonlit night when I finally saw

Tipsy. She was dressed in red Pakistani bridal clothes, and was sitting on a stage in front of a huge crowd. She had a female guard on either side of her. She stood up when she saw me and shouted, 'Oh Frank, you came for me…' but before she could finish the sentence, the guards grabbed her and forced her to sit. Just then, drums burst loudly into life, and a moment or so later I saw the drummers. On either side of them was a flag bearer, behind them were two men who were naked from their waists upwards, and behind them were two important looking bearded men, dressed in black, with black turbans on their heads. I would very soon learn that these two men were competing for Tipsy.

The flag bearers came towards the stage, a slightly raised piece of ground, turned around and faced the audience. The semi-naked men each stopped in front of a flag. The men in black sat down on large carved chairs.

The crowd was divided into men and women by large white sheets of cloth that hung down from ropes tied to trees. Rows of men were pounding something in large stone mortars with long wooden pestles. Behind them, other men were preparing goats on spits for roasting.

A guard pointed towards a white plastic chair furthest away from Tipsy on the stage, and ordered, 'Sir be seated!'

I sat down and looked out at a group of elders, all dressed in white clothes and white turbans. They sat on a carpeted section of the ground at the front of the crowd.

Another man, also naked from the waist upwards, materialized from somewhere. He was a tall light-skinned man with a stern face. He carried a leather slap-paddle in his right hand. He waved across to the elders with the open palm of his left hand and said, 'By the wisdom of our Jirga, oh Council of Elders,' and then paused and pointed to Tipsy, adding, 'this white woman,' he paused again, bowed towards the men in black turbans and said, raising his head, 'she is for one of you tonight.' He clapped his hands and added, 'Let the competition begin.'

This can't be real, I thought, this can't be a competition for who gets Tipsy.

The two men who were naked from the waist up stepped forward. Their oiled bodies shone in the moonlight.

'You know, Ustad Lither,' Kameena said. A broad smile flashed across his dark-skinned face. He had shoulder-length curly black hair.

'Yes, Kameena.'

'After his death, General Zia goes to meet God, and gets in line behind all the leaders of the world. Even the Indians are there. God gets up and embraces each leader in turn. But when General Zia gets to him, God does not stand up but offers Zia his hand instead.

"Almighty, why is it that when you met other leaders, you stood up and embraced them, but you only offered to shake my hand?"

"You are such a bastard," God replied, "if I stood up to embrace you, you might end up stealing my chair."'

Lither turned to the other storyteller. Apart from having a shining bald head, he could have been Kameena's twin brother.

'And you know, Master Lither,' the other storyteller said.

'Yes, Kanjar,' Lither replied.

'Aren't our leaders all spawned by limp dicks?' Kanjar asked.

Lither hit him with the slap-paddle.

'You never know whose dick is up whose arse, or who will fuck who for how long,' Kanjar said, and just as Lither was about to hit him again, he said, 'Let me explain. In 1976, General Zia is appointed as Army Chief of Staff by ZAB, Prime Minister Zulfikar

Ali Bhutto, the father of Benazir Bhutto. General Zia overthrows Zulfikar Ali Butto and has him executed. And then, when General Zia is blown to bits, he is not alone, he has with him, as they say in English, *Very Important Pakistanis*, lots of VIPs, and also the American Ambassador to Pakistan, Arnold Raphel, and he too dies.' Kanjar continued, 'And Amereekans, they loved General Zia at that time, of course. And then later on, ZAB's daughter, Benazir Bhutto, becomes a Prime Minister, and then she herself is assassinated in Rawalpindi in 2007, and then her husband, who takes a ten percent cut on every government contract, Mister Ten Percent, becomes the President of the country.' Turning his face towards Lither, Kanjar asks, 'Do you remember that dog, Mister Ten Percent?'

'How dare you insult dogs,' Lither said, whacking Kanjar.

'I'm going to talk about his wife.' Kanjar protested. 'After her death, Benazir Bhutto goes straight to hell, where all the Pakistani rulers are standing up to their necks in shit. She looks around, but cannot see her father. Filled with happiness, she mocks General Zia, "You hanged an innocent man. My dad was honest and has gone to heaven."

General Zia replies, "I'm standing on the bastard's shoulders.'"

I didn't know whether to laugh or cry at the scene that was unfolding in front of my eyes, especially once I had worked out what the stage names meant: *Lither* is a slap-paddle; and *kameena* is a pejorative form of *kami* for a worker; as is *kanjar,* meaning a dancer, which in its feminine form implies a prostitute.

Apart from a kidnapped white man and woman, and two big bearded men and the Jirga, the rest of the set up was typical of local theatrical performances known as *tamashas*. Over a number of trips to this country, I had seen many a *tamasha*, and had been told that the slap-paddle didn't really cause pain, but just made a lot of noise.

I was regretting my decision to have followed Tipsy to Pakistan, and thought back to a few hours earlier.

*****

After checking in to my hotel in Islamabad, I had taken a taxi to Jabra Chouk, and gone into the huge complex of the Faisal Mosque, where General Zia,

Pakistan's late dictator, is buried in a shrine-like mausoleum. Given what we had discovered, this is where Tipsy would certainly have come.

Unlike my previous visits, this time a policeman was guarding the entrance to the grave. He smiled as he saw me walking towards him.

When I got closer to him, I said in Pothohari, the local language (which both Tipsy and I speak fluently), 'Pakistan is going through bad times when the graves of the dead have to be protected.'

The policeman stood to attention, looking shocked. A typical local reaction when they realise I can speak their language.

'You must have lived here all your life to speak our language like you do,' the policeman replied, brushing his waxed moustache with the back of his hand.

'No, sir, in Birmingham,' I replied.

The policeman looked a bit confused and said, 'Manchester United?'

Again, not an untypical response.

'How long has there been a guard on the grave of General Zia?' I asked.

'Ever since people started coming here to piss on it,' he replied, walking away towards a group of his colleagues who were sitting in the shade of the mosque.

As he was walking away, I asked him, 'Sir, is it true

when they say that only General Zia's jaw is buried here?'

The policeman turned around, looked at me, twirled his moustache and replied, 'Jaw, hands, testicles, who knows?'

I noticed a man squatting in the shade of the arches to the entrance of General Zia's mausoleum. He was staring at me. He had a black beard, prayer beads in his hand, and wore a green turban. He looked like one of the official guardian types of these sorts of places.

'Are you the custodian of General Zia's shrine?' I asked him.

He looked at me with his sharp green eyes and continued praying.

I had asked in Pothohari, but he wasn't surprised.

'Once a year, I come here to spend the afternoons praying,' he eventually replied. He raised both his hands in prayer, looked skywards and added, 'Ya Allah, don't ever let the bastard get out of hell.'

He had a multicoloured scarf wrapped around his wrist. It was similar to the one Tipsy often wore in Birmingham.

I showed him a photograph of Tipsy and said, 'I am looking for this friend of mine, she might have come here.'

Green Eyes saw me looking at the scarf, and replied, 'She has gone to find him. *He* will be at the Zia Mela, the Zia festival, tonight.'

Even as I agreed to go to the festival with him, I felt it was the wrong thing to do; and around three hours into the journey along dirt roads, I realised what a terrible mistake I had made, when he introduced himself as Akber Zeb Junior, the very man who had sent me the Facebook link. He was sitting next to his driver in the front and I sat in the middle, between them and two armed guards in the rear, in his seven-seater four-by-four.

*****

Kameena's loud voice stopped my thoughts when he said, 'After the death of his wife, Benazir Bhutto, Zardari becomes the President of Pakistan. He is in the Presidential limousine being driven by his driver. He is going through a poor neighbourhood when his driver accidentally runs over a small dog, a puppy. Zardari orders the driver, "Go find out whose dog has been killed and we will give them some compensation."

The driver goes off into the neighbourhood and takes a very long time to come back. When he does eventually return, he is adorned with garlands of flowers and hundreds of people are dancing behind him. He bids them farewell and returns to his master's car.

"Why are they all so happy?" Zardari asks.

"I don't know, sir. I just told them that I was President Zardari's driver, and it was me who killed the son of a bitch.'"

As Kameena was reaching the end of his story, he quickly ran off before Lither could hit him, hid behind Kanjar, and protested, 'Sir, I haven't finished my story!'

'Hurry up!' Lither orders.

Kameena steps forward and asks Lither, 'Master, you know how times are bad nowadays, with thieves and bandits everywhere?'

'Yes,' Lither replies,

'Well, President Zardari's driver is going along the main road when armed bandits stop the car. One of the bandits puts a gun to Zardari's head and says, "Give us your money."

Zardari is enraged and shouts at the bandit, "Don't you realize that I am the President of Pakistan."

"In that case," says the robber, "give us our money.'"

Lither looked at the audience, and then at the storytellers. He rubbed the slap-paddle over each story-teller's shoulders and asked, in a slow menacing voice, 'I want you to tell me some of the good deeds of General Zia.'

The storytellers looked at each other, dumbfounded.

Kanjar's face suddenly lit up with a smile and he said, 'He taught us we were Muslims.'

'We weren't kafirs before he came, you son of a camel,' Lither replied, striking him.

'And he legitimized sex,' Kanjar said.

'You mean the whole of Pakistan was fucking illegitimate before?' Lither said.

Kanjar raised his hand and replied, 'Let me explain, Master Lither.'

'It better be a good explanation. You cannot insult a whole nation and expect to keep the skin on your back.'

Kanjar turned his back on Lither and said to the audience, 'It was in 1979 when General Zia legitimized sex in Pakistan. He gave us the Hadood Ordinance, the Sex Ordinance. He gave us the Kazis and the Kazi courts.

The first case to be brought in front of the Kazi Courts involved an Imam and a woman who were accused of having sex outside marriage. There was, as required, a male witness to this of course. But he had no tongue and was, unfortunately, dumb. So the Kazi ordered the presence of a translator who could read sign language.

The Kazi calls the dumb witness to the stand and asks him, "What did you see?"

The witness points to his chest, places the first two fingers of his right hand on the stand and walks them forward.'

Kanjar stops, opens the palm of his left hand and walks two fingers of his right hand a couple of times on his palm, and then says, 'The witness then mimes taking off his clothes and makes a series of complicated hand signals.

The translator translates for the Kazi, "I saw a woman come into the room. She walked across the hall and entered the bedroom, took her clothes off and jumped on the bed."

The Kazi then asks the witness, "Is the woman in this court?"

The witness points to the only woman in the court.

"What happened next?' the Kazi asks.

The witness rubs his hand across his beard, places two fingers on the stand and walks the fingers forward. He then mimes taking off his clothes and makes a series of complicated hand signals.

The translator explains, "Then a bearded man followed the woman, took his clothes off and jumped on the bed."

The Kazi asks the witness, "Is the man in the court?"

The witness points to the Imam standing next to the woman.

"What happened next?" the Kazi asks.

The witness clapped.'

Kanjar stopped speaking and started clapping his hands. He then put both hands together, making a series of noises with them. He put the middle finger of his right hand into the clenched fist of his left, pushed it in and out a few times, and then waved his hands in the air and panted. Finally, he raised his hands up in the air before dropping them to his sides and said, 'Then the translator explained to the Kazi, "They fucked for two hours without stopping, as God is my witness."

"Two hours! Are you sure?" the Kazi asks. "Without a break?"

The witness goes into a deep thoughtful silence and then shrugs his shoulders, showing three fingers.

The translator explains, "Maybe three."

"Ya Allah! Maybe three hours! Are you absolutely sure?" the Kazi asks.

The witness nods.

"And what happened next?" the Kazi asks.

The witness touches his chest,'

Kanjar stops, opens the palm of his left hand and places the index and middle fingers of his right hand on the palm of his left. The fingers are spread wide apart. He walks these ever so slowly across his palm, whilst miming great soreness and effort with his mouth and breathing, and then says, 'The translator explained that the woman left.

"What happened next?" the Kazi asks.

The witness rubs his beard,'

Kanjar stops again, and then places the same fingers of his right hand on the palm of his left again, but this time they are not spread apart. He walks these ever so slowly across his palm as well and, as before, mimes great soreness and effort with his mouth and breathing, and says, 'The translator explained that the Imam came stumbling out.

"What were you doing all this time?" the Kazi asked the witness.'

Kanjar turned to the audience, opened the palm of his left hand again and showed it to everyone. He then placed the first three fingers of his right hand on the palm of his left. The centre finger was erect.

There was pandemonium in the audience, with people laughing and shouting, and celebratory gun-fire.

'General Zia is sinking in quicksand and fighting for his life,' Kameena said. 'He is sinking deeper and deeper and calls out, "Help! Save me! Can anyone save me?"

A voice from above replies, "God here, General Zia. I will save you, but on one condition."

"Any condition, Almighty! Any!"

"You have to tell the truth," the voice says.

"Can anyone else save me?" General Zia calls out.'

'What a bastard you are, insulting our great leader,' Lither said, hitting Kameena with the slap-paddle.

'Master Lither, please hit that ungrateful son of a bitch again,' Kanjar said, pointing to Kameena, 'for not praising the beauty of General Zia's wife.'

'You do it then,' Lither said, raising the slap-paddle.

'Once, all Pakistan's top generals were in a meeting at the General Headquarters, the GHQ in Rawalpindi,' Kanjar said, 'all listening intently to

General Zia. Mister Arnold Raphel, the American Ambassador to Pakistan, was sitting next to the sharp-tongued General Chisti when Zia's wife walked in.'

'Why have you brought the Americans into this?' Lither asked, striking Kanjar with the slap-paddle.

Kameena stepped forward, saying, 'If you don't mind, perhaps I can be of assistance here.'

Lither folded his arms in front of his chest and nodded.

'You see Master Lither, as you know, I can read English and am good at counting' Kameena said.

'What baqwas, what rubbish, are you coming out with?' Lither said, whacking Kameena.

'Well, sir, you see the first letter, 'A', if we take one of them, then three times, then that makes AAA, which equals 'Triple A' : America, Army, Allah.'

Lither struck him three times and Kameena protested, 'But sir, you have not let me finish.'

Lither stepped back from him and Kameena continued, 'As you know, most countries own an Army, but our Army owns the country.'

Lither hit Kameena, saying, 'How dare you put America before Allah! Just tell us about the adventures of our departed General Zia.'

'General Zia goes to Balouchistan dressed as an ordinary man, so that he can understand why the Balouchis have lost respect for the Pakistani flag,' Kameena said. 'He goes up to a poor Balouchi and asks, "Do you know what the historical significance of the Pakistani flag is?"

"No," the Balouchi replies.

"Do you know how many sacrifices were made for this flag?" General Zia asks.

"No."

"Do you know what the colours of the flag represent?" General Zia asks.

"No."

"The crescent and the green are for Islam, and the white for all our minorities," General Zia explains.

"Ah, now I understand why the danda, the pole, is always shoved up the white."'

Just as Lither was about to hit Kameena, Kanjar stepped forward and said, 'As I was saying, all our brave generals were meeting in the Army's GHQ, and General Zia was talking about something very important, and everyone was listening intently, when his wife walked in. And Ambassador Raphel whispered to General Chisti, "Who the hell is this woman?"

"Shh, Sir! That's General Zia's wife."

"If General Zia can fuck her, then Pakistan is no problem," says the American Ambassador.'

'That General Chisti, Master Lither,' Kameena said as soon as Kanjar stopped, 'he really was a sister-fucking idiot, he was.'

'How dare you swear at your brave General,' Lither replied, hitting him.

'What you may not know,' Kameena said, rubbing his back, 'is that General Chisti and General Zia were the best of friends. General Zia trusted him more than anyone else.

One day, our brave General Chisti is walking past a graveyard and hears a voice, "Bring me a horse."

General Chisti runs to General Zia and tells him what has just happened.

"General Chisti, there are no voices in graveyards. The dead are dead. We tell this sort of thing to ignorant villagers. Go back again to the same graveyard, and I guarantee you there will be no voice."

General Chisti goes back, and the voice shouts angrily, "Bring me a horse!"

A terrified General Chisti bolts back to General Zia and tells him it happened again.

"You are hearing things," General Zia reprimands him, 'and stop drinking so much whisky."

To prove his point, General Zia accompanies General Chisti to the graveyard. When both Generals reach the graveyard, the voice is furious and shouts, "General Chisti, I asked for a horse not a mother-fucking donkey!'"

Kameena smiles at Kanjar, who says, 'You know, I used to work as General Zia's cook, and that day when he came home, he was fuming. He ran around the house searching everywhere for something, mumbling, "Everyone is fucking my wife." As you know, he was a very clever man. He read my thoughts, well a part of them anyway, and said, "Oh, you want to know how I know?" which, of course, was the part that he read correctly; the other was closer to what the Ambassador had said. And so General Zia replied to my thoughts, "The Americans know everything."

From that day onwards, General Zia begins to suspect that someone among the top Pakistani Generals is sleeping with his wife. He gets more and more worried the closer he gets to an important foreign trip to America. Before he goes off on this visit to the US, he makes me help him make a chastity belt out of blades, and he puts this on his wife.

When General Zia comes back from his trip, he makes all the top Generals stand in a line. He goes up to the first and asks, "Did you sleep with my wife?"

"I swear on the Almighty, I was awake all night," the first General answers.

General Zia orders the General to drop his pants. He does. His dick is shredded. General Zia orders him executed.

Then General Zia goes up to the second General and asks, "Did you sleep with my wife?"

The second General shakes his head. General Zia orders him to drop his pants as well. His dick is also cut to pieces. General Zia orders him to be executed also.

Eventually, it is the turn of General Chisti, who drops his trousers before being asked.
General Chisti's dick is still there.

General Zia hugs General Chisti, saying, "Shukr Alhamdolillah, Thanks be to the Almighty. You alone have stood by me. Ask what you would like, and your wish will be granted."

But General Chisti lowers his head.

"Ask for anything you want. It is yours," General Zia insists.

General Chishti mumbles unintelligibly.

"Go on, my trusted friend, what is your deepest desire," General Zia says. "All you have to do is say the word."

But General Chisti continues to shake his head, roll his eyes and mumble. General Zia gets angry and orders, "Come on man, open your mouth and move that tongue of yours."

General Chisti opens his mouth. His tongue is shredded.'

Lither got a packet of cigarettes from the front pocket of his shalvaar, his trousers, took a match out of the packet and struck it on Kanjar's bald head. The match burst into flames and Lither lit his cigarette, inhaled deeply and then blew smoke rings out of his mouth. As he did this, Kanjar said, 'Master Lither.'

'Yes, Kanjar.'

'They say, if you don't have enough shit in your arse, don't invite the crows,' Kanjar said. 'A smoke for this Kanjar would be welcomed.'

Lither hit him, and then gave him a cigarette. As Kanjar toe-chained his cigarette from Lither's, Kameena said, 'Master Lither.'

'Yes, Kameena.'

'Do you think I am not even worth *Chiri di chut da*

chaleeswaan hissa, one 40th of the cunt of a sparrow?' Kameena asked.

'Why do you ask?'

'You gave that Kanjar, who fucked his own mother to be born, a cigarette, but not me.'

Lither hit Kameena, who, like Kanjar, took a cigarette and a light from Lither.

'Master Lither,' Kanjar said.

'Yes, Kanjar.'

'I cannot let that Kameena insult my mother.'

'What are you going to do about it, then?' Lither asked.

Kanjar turned to Kameena and said, 'You'll be fingered so badly, you will miss the dick.'

I just did not understand why anyone would laugh at this, it made no sense.

Kameena raised his head arrogantly at Kanjar, and posed for the audience briefly before saying, 'He couldn't get fucked with a fistful of 50s in a whorehouse.'

Kanjar turned towards the Jirga and said, 'My noble sirs, as you know, this Kameena went to work in Dubai and made a load of money. Just like lots of men from your villages, they come back and build houses, sometimes bigger than their chiefs.'

Lither smacked Kanjar and said, 'Stop giving a speech.'

'I was just going to say,' Kanjar replied, 'But no matter how big the balls grow, they are still under the dick.'

Kanjar moved away, scratching his groin.

'They say,' Kameena said, pointing to Kanjar's groin, 'If hair was any good, it would not grow between the legs.'

'Pubes cannot block the path of the dick,' Kanjar snapped back.

Kanjar placed his chin in his hand, looked around in thoughtful silence for a moment and then said, 'Let me tell you, my friends, my sages and, of course, you Master Lither. Let me take you back to that fateful day this poor nation of ours was bereft of our beloved General Zia. And to the days when our wise re-emerging Prime Minister, Nawaz Sharif, was a young man. So let me take you back to that fateful day when General Zia's plane was blown out of the sky.

The Americans are pissed off with the Pakistani military for the death of Arnold Raphel, the US Ambassador to Pakistan, who was travelling with Zia at the time the plane was blown up. The Americans declare the place where the debris lands as a crime scene, and send a team of US investigators to the place.

Nawaz Sharif takes the American investigators to the site of the event. Bits of human bodies are littered all over the place. A limb here, a torso there.'

Kameena bent down, pretended to pick something up and said, 'Nawaz Sharif bends down, picks something up and slips it into his pocket. Ah, but you know these Americans are really clever, and a sharp-eyed investigator sees Nawaz Sharif doing this and asks him, "What did you just pick up?"

"Nothing, sir,"

"Take your hand out of your pocket and show me what you have picked up."'

Kameena waved his clenched fist in front of the audience and said, 'So, Nawaz Sharif puts his hand into his pocket and pulls out two bits of fleshy things.

"What are these?" the American asks.

"These are General Zia's testicles, sir," Nawaz Sharif answers, "I just want to keep them as a memento of our great leader."

The American looks at all the bits and pieces of human remains, and asks Nawaz Sharif, "In all this mess, how in God's name do you know they are General Zia's?"

"I spent 11 years kissing them, sir," Nawaz Sharif replies.'

As soon as Kameena finished, Kanjar said, 'After the American investigator puts General Zia's testicles into a bag, Nawaz Sharif walks up to a pair of severed hands. The hands are clasping a pair of testicles. Nawaz Sharif stands to attention and salutes.

"Why, Mister Sharif, are you Pakistanis so fascinated by testicles? Why are you saluting these?" the American asks.

"I am not saluting the testicles, sir. I am saluting General Zia's hands," Nawaz Sharif replies.

"How in God's name do you know these are General Zia's hands?" the American asks.

"Sir, who else would be holding Ambassador Raphel's balls," Nawaz Sharif replies.'

Then Kameena said, 'An angel is looking at a coffin with General Zia's bits and pieces in it. The Almighty says to the angel, "This man did terrible things to Pakistan. Bring him to me, but along the way get a shoe and spank his arse."

The angel comes down, gets a shoe and starts to spank General Zia's arse. But instead of crying, General Zia's mouth starts laughing. The angel gets angry and hits him harder and harder, but General Zia's mouth does not stop laughing. Eventually, the poor angel gets tired and asks General Zia, "Why are you laughing when I am spanking your buttocks so hard with this shoe?"

"The buttocks belong to Ambassador Raphel." General Zia replies.'

Part II:
Rebellion of
Native Women

Something truly astounding happened. There was a commotion in the audience, mostly from the side of the cloth partition where the women sat.

A woman stood up. She wore a short-sleeved shiny green top, and a brown dress embroidered with golden vegetable patterns, popular in Kashmir and this part of the world. But for her eyes, her face was covered by a scarf matching the colours of her dress.

Lither looked surprised.

The woman uncovered her face.

I was expecting a gasp from the audience, but nothing. She stepped forward, with careful and deliberate footsteps.

'My name is Khairaan, and I have had enough of this, this bullshit,' Khairaan said, striding towards Lither. He stepped back.

She was a tall dark-skinned woman, closer to the Dravidian stock than the majority Aryans of this region. She had shining bright eyes, perfectly set in a handsome face, not untypical of the transgenders of Pakistan.

Kanjar and Kameena stared at her with open mouths. Snatching the slap-paddle out of Lither's hand, she turned to the male section of the audience and asked, 'So, you think that whilst you men fight over us women …' They went silent as she paused. She turned to the women and asked, nodding at the men, 'And they think we will sit around, fighting over them, whilst they fight over us!'

Khairaan continued, 'They want to fight over a white woman, well let us have the white man; he's got something we might want.'

The women burst out laughing.

'A gora for me,' a woman shouted from the shadows.

'You're an old hag. Let us young ones have him first,' a different woman replied.

Kameena asked Khairaan, 'Why don't we share the white man?'

'He's not a kebab,' Khairaan replied, whacking Kameena with the slap-paddle.

'But some of us men might want what he's got as well,' Kanjar added.

'Let the men have his behind,' a woman shouted out.

'Some of them won't be satisfied with just that,' another woman's voice answered.

The women laughed and screamed. The men remained silent.

This absurd drama into which I had been plunged was worse than the theatre of the absurd, I thought. How the hell had I got myself into this shite. If Tipsy was so reckless as to come out to this godforsaken country, why the fuck did I have to follow her out here? Then I looked across at her, and she looked like a fragile flower in a field of wild thorns. I knew then that I was deeply in love with her. Then I smiled at the thought of seeing a headline of my demise in a Brit tabloid: *Filth Collecting Professor Goes Down Without Getting Laid.*

Unless you can find a way out of this, Frank, I thought, either both of us, or at least one of us, is not leaving alive.

There was another disturbance, this time among the Jirga. Khairaan nodded towards someone in there, folded her arms across her front and waited. There were loud whispers and some noises of disapproval. Eventually, Khairaan was beckoned towards the Jirga. She stepped forward and bent down towards a tribal elder in the centre of the front row. A restless hum buzzed over the men in the audience as she did this. The women remained silent. As Khairaan straightened up again, everything went quiet and she said, 'I too am going to compete, and if I win, I will take the white man.'

I stood up and shouted, 'No one is getting my arse,' but the women were making so much noise, I am not sure anyone heard me.

Khairaan raised her hand, and suddenly the silence returned. A guard rushed at me, gun in hand, and I shouted, 'I choose who gets my arse!'

Khairaan looked at me derisively and nodded at the guard, who pointed at my chair with his gun. I sat down.

With the slap-paddle dangling in her hand, she walked slowly towards Kameena and asked, 'Is it true what they say in Turkey, "An idle shopkeeper weighs his balls?"'

Kameena pointed at me and said, 'They also say, the luckless Bedouin gets fucked by a polar bear in the desert.'

I felt scared, realising what it was he was implying in relation to me.

Khairaan hit Kameena, and he said, 'I am as old as your father, you know.'

'And?' Khairaan asked.

'I could have been your father if that dog had not got there first,' Kameena replied.

Whilst everyone else laughed, I was terrified. I took a deep breath and thought *don't let the natives see you scared*. And then it occurred to me that, like Khairaan, I too could fight for what I wanted. At least that way I had a chance.

Meanwhile Khairaan turned towards the women and said, 'You know, girls, how these men, when they talk to each other, they all claim to be stallions. But we know the truth, don't we?'

'The only time mine stands up straight is when he goes to the mosque to pray,' a voice from among the women said.

'Shakarallamdulillah, thanks be to the Lord,' another woman replied, 'at least he manages to stand up.'

'Mine doesn't know how to pray,' a different woman shouted.

'You know, girls?' Khairaan asked, and then answered herself, 'when men bend down and see four testicles between their legs, they shouldn't think they are *superman*.'

Khairaan used the English word '*superman*'. Hardly surprising, I thought, as there was no concept of superman in any Pakistani language. I was trying to work out what Khairaan meant, when a woman from the crowd shouted out, 'Maybe some of them become *supermen* only then.'

Once again the women roared with laughter but the men remained silent, and Khairaan continued, 'But let me tell you about this Imam who teaches children how to read the Holy Quran. He has an itchy arse and can't stop scratching it, even whilst leading the prayers or whilst teaching children to read the Holy Quran.

People refuse to pray behind the Imam, and parents stop sending their children to be taught by him.

When the money runs out, the Imam's wife says to him, "Light of my eyes, we have no food left in the house. You must see the Hakim, the doctor, and see if he can get rid of your itch."

The Imam listens to his wife and goes to see the Hakim. The Hakim rubs a special ointment into the Imam's arse and, Subhan Allah, Praise be to God, the Imam's itch goes away. He starts leading the prayers again, and parents send their children back to him to learn the Holy Quran.

After a few weeks, a wise parent notices the Imam rubbing his behind on the ground whilst giving a lesson to the children, and she runs to the Imam's wife and says, "Sister, sister, your husband is getting his itch again. You must do whatever you did before and nip it in the bud, and stop him from scratching his arse, or else this time we will not send our children back."

The wife goes to her husband and says, "Jan-e-mann, beloved, parents have started to complain again."

The Imam lowers his head.

"Did the Hakim not say to rub some ointment in your behind whenever the itch returns?" the wife asks.

The Imam nods his head.'

Khairaan pauses, cusps her right hand and pretends to scoop up some ointment, saying, 'The wife gets the ointment,' and then with her middle finger protruding forwards, Khairaan moves her hand in an upwards gesture whilst saying, 'And then, like this, the wife starts to rub it in and out of the Imam's arse, in and out, up and down.

After a little while, the Imam says, "You aren't rubbing it properly."

"But hayati, my life, I am doing my best."

"Rub harder," the Imam says.'

Khairaan then makes a loud groaning noise, as she pretends to put more effort into the rubbing and says, 'The wife tries harder, and asks, "Is this better, my husband?"

"No. The Hakim did it better, and I really enjoyed it."

"Ya Allah, give this woman more strength!" the wife calls out.

"I can feel your left hand on the back of my left shoulder, wife. Where is your right hand?" the Imam asks.

"I am rubbing the ointment into your arse with my right hand, my husband."

"But the Hakim had both his hands on my shoulders," the Imam says.'

Without waiting, Khairaan launches into another story.

'One day, a young man who has got into the bad habit of fucking cats comes along to this Imam and wants some advice. The young man wants to be rid of his habit.

The Imam listens to him, gives him an amulet and says, "Pray five times a day and wear this amulet, and bring a goat as an offering to my house tomorrow and, God willing, you will be cured of this disgusting habit very quickly."

The young man follows the advice and, Shukaral-hamdollillah, Thanks be to God, he is cured.

A few days later, there is a knock on the young man's door. The youth opens the door. The Imam is standing there. He is bleeding from the head and face.

"Dear Imam, how can I ever repay you for helping me quit my terrible habit?" the young man asks.

"Just tell me how you kept hold of the mother-fucking cats.'"

And then Khairaan turns to the women.

'As you know, sisters, these men think, we just wait at home for them to come home for their couple of minutes worth of pleasure.'

The women clapped and laughed. When they calmed down Khairaan continued, 'Well as you know, before coming here I grew up in Lebanon, which is a small country about the size of the district of Jhelum. In Lebanon, there is a famous man called Abu el Abid. He dies, and the police find his testicles and ask Imm el Abid to identify them.

'She goes to the police station and a row of testicles are placed on a table. She points to the first pair and says, 'Not his,' and then she points to the second pair and says, 'Not his,' and then the third pair and says, 'Not from our village.'

Whilst the women stand up, clap and whistle, the men sit stiffly. Khairaan waits a moment or so and then says, 'As Abu el Abid is being taken for burial, he suddenly gets an enormous erection.'

Khairaan moves her hands to show the size of the erection and continues, 'The funeral procession stops and someone asks the Sheikh, those that we call Mullahs, what should be done. He examines Abu el Abid to make sure he has not miraculously come alive, but he is dead as dead.

As this is happening, a woman runs to Imm el Abid, Abu el Abid's wife, and says to her, "Sister, sister, Abu el Abid has just got an enormous erection, the biggest I've ever seen."

Imm al Abid, who is in her house in mourning, replies, "That is a miracle indeed, if you've seen Abu el Abid's erection as well. I only ever saw it once."

"Naouzbillah, we seek refuge in Allah. No, sister, I have only just seen it now, as I was walking past his funeral," the woman replies.

"You selfish bastard, Abu el Abid," Imm el Abid wails, "all these years I had to make do with droopy sons of bitches, and here you are getting an erection on your way to the grave."

Meanwhile, a number of Sheikhs have got together to decide what to do with Abu el Abid's erect dick.

"He must have been an evil bastard to be punished like this," says the first Sheikh.

"Who could call getting such a big hard-on a punishment?" asks the second, "Mashallah, God has willed, this is a gift from Him. For any man to be bestowed with an erection like this just before his burial, Abu el Abid is surely destined for heaven.

"Let's not keep the hoors waiting and just bury him," says the third, who was blind.

"But the issue before is," says the first Sheikh, "that every Muslim must have a ghusal, be cleansed, before he goes to meet his maker. But as we know, anyone who gets an erection, for the erect dick can't help leaking, is no longer clean and, therefore, a dead man who gets one is also not clean and, therefore, we have to wash him again. But are we allowed to actually bury a man with his dick standing? I have not come across anything in the Holy Scriptures."

"Chop it off," says the second Sheikh.

"What about the poor hoors?" asks the blind one.

Unable to solve this delicate issue, the Sheikhs decide to go and seek the advice of the most senior Sheikh in the land, who, after listening to the problem, gives his fatwa, "Cut the dick off, but before you do that, you must get his wife's permission."

The Sheikhs send a messenger to Imm el Abid, and she replies, "If the big Sheikh says this must be done, then it must be done. Besides, it has never been much good to me.'"

Khairaan stopped, made a pretend sawing action with her hands, and continued, 'And so Abu el Abid's dick is sawn off. The Sheiks once again start arguing. This time it's about what to do with the dismembered dick.

"Abu el Abid has changed the meaning of resurrection," says the first.

"His dick must be burnt," says the second.

"Muslims cannot be burnt," says the blind one. "All his parts have to be buried in the ground."

The first Sheikh puts Abu el Abid's dick next to his feet.

"We must not put the dick at his feet. They say paradise is to be found under the feet of the mother. What will people say about what is to be found under the feet of the father?" the second Sheikh objects, and puts the dick on top of Abu el Abid's right shoulder.

"La Hawla Wala Quwwata Illa Billah, there is no power but that of Allah," the second Sheikh objects. "The angel who records our good deeds sits on the right shoulder." And he insists, "We must put the dick on Abu el Abid's left shoulder."

"There is also an angel who sits on the left shoulder, who records the misdeeds," the blind Sheikh says, "but he is still an angel. I say we bury Abu el Abid's dick in a separate grave."

"A man cannot have two graves," insists the first Sheikh.

So the Sheikhs return to the senior Sheikh and ask for his advice, and he pronounces another fatwa, "Stick the dick up his arse, in that way he can be buried whole. But you must ask permission from his wife."

Another messenger is sent to Imm el Abid, who replies, "If the big Sheikh says this must be done, then it must be done, but I want to be present and hold Abu el Abid's hand when you do this."

Abu el Abid is turned on his stomach. Imm el Abid holds his hand.'

Khairaan stops, and with her hands pretends to hold a huge penis and slowly push it forward, saying, 'And so, Abu el Abid's dick begins to be pushed up his behind.' She stops, claps her hands, and adds, 'When the last bit of it slips into his arse, a tear comes out of Abu el Abid's eye. Imm el Abid leans over to him and whispers in his ear, "I told you it hurts."'

'How shall I address you?' Kameena asked Khairaan, brushing his hair off his face, 'As Madam, or Sister?'

'You may call me *Sister*,' Khairaan replied 'And what shall I call you?'

'Sister-fucker,' Kameena replied.

'Inshahallah, it will rain dicks,' Khairaan cursed Kameena, 'and your mother's pussy will be on the roof.'

Khairaan hits Kanjar on the back and he says, 'A blind Imam is sitting on his own in the mosque, praying. "Ya Allah, people ask you for wealth, big houses and sons, but me, this blind servant of yours, this is the first time I have asked you for anything. Almighty, send me just one hoor who fucks me every night.

A horny farmer is walking by and hears the Imam asking the Almighty for a hoor. The farmer goes into the mosque and says, "Hello there human, I am your Lord. I have heard your prayer and will send you a hoor."

"Allah O Akber," the Imam replies, "when, Almighty, when?"

The farmer replies, (Kanjar said this in a high-pitched voice), "I am a hoor and he has sent me to fuck you senseless."

Before the blind Imam has time to digest his good fortune, the farmer grabs hold of him, turns him over and fucks him. This happens for three days. On the fourth day, the Imam is tired and shouts, "Ya Allah, have the Imams from the other mosques died?"'

'Sister Khairaan,' Kanjar continued, 'These women are discussing something private and laughing when one of them notices a young man, a stranger to these parts, eavesdropping on their conversation. The woman nods disapprovingly at him and asks, "Why do men's ears stand up when they hear us talking to each other."

'The young stranger asks in reply, "Is that what you call ears around here?"

'The Imam in our mosque, sister Khairaan, is not blind,' said Kameena

'Oh yes,' replied Khairaan.

'In his Friday Khutbah, his sermon, the Imam tells

the congregation, "If any of you see a visit from the devil at night, if any of you have a wet dream, then as god-fearing Muslims, you must go to the person you have seen in your dreams and tell them to have a shower."

The next morning there is a knock on the Imam's door. He opens the door. A young man is standing outside, who says to the Imam, "Could you please tell your younger daughter to have a shower."

"Thank you my son, may God bless you," the Imam replies.

The following morning there is another knock on the Imam's door. The Imam opens it. It is the same young man, who says, "Could you please ask your elder daughter to have a shower."

"Yes, thank you," the Imam replies.

And the next morning there is another knock on the Imam's door. It is the same youth, who says, "Could you please ask your wife to have a shower."

"Yes," the Imam replies, slamming the door shut.

The next day there is yet another knock on the Imam's door. He opens the door and shouts at the youth, "I have had a shower."'

'And what about the Imam of your village,' Khairaan asked Kanjar.

'Our Sheikh, our Imam, gets married, sister Khairaan. Each morning the mother of the bride telephones her and asks, " I am getting old. I need a grandchild. Did you fuck last night?"

And the daughter replies, "No. He is not interested in sex."

This goes on for a number of years. The mother gets desperate and asks around the Sheikh's neighbourhood about what turns her son-in-law on. She discovers that he gets aroused by corpses.

So the mother phones her daughter and says, "Daughter, tomorrow morning get up before your husband wakes up, go outside your bedroom, lie down on the floor and pretend to be dead."

The dutiful daughter does as she is advised. The Sheikh, seeing his wife dead on the floor, gets horny and fucks her. The next morning, the daughter tells her mother the good news. The mother advises the daughter to do this every day.

A month later the mother telephones her daughter, "Daughter, I have bad news for you. Your father just died."

The daughter quickly replies, "Fuck him, fuck him, he will come alive."'

'Sister Khairaan,' Kanjar continued, 'this Sheikh

becomes one of the wisest in the world. People come from everywhere to seek his advice. One day, a poor man comes to the Sheikh and says to him, "Honourable Sheikh, I have a big problem."

"Tell me of your problem and, Inshahallah, I might be able to offer you some advice that will ease your burden."

"I want to divorce my wife," the man replies.

"A divorce is permissible, but remember that women have rights in Islam. You must have a valid reason."

"Her pussy is so big, I don't enjoy sex with her."

"How big?"

"I am embarrassed to tell you, Sheikh."

"Try to show me."

"But she is my wife!"

"I mean show me with your hands."

The man cusps his hands in front of the Sheikh.

On seeing the cusped hands, the Sheikh shakes his head, saying, "This is a really big problem. I cannot suggest a solution. You have to take the advice of a more senior Sheikh than me."

"But you are the most senior of Sheikhs."

"Get out!" the Sheikh orders.

The man leaves, feeling dejected. A few months later, the man ends up praying next to the Sheikh.

At first the Sheikh does not realise the man is next to him, but when the Sheikh turns his head to the left after concluding his prayer, he recognises the man and immediately goes into a fit of rage and starts beating him up. People in the mosque quickly intervene and restrain the Sheikh.

"Forgive me, Ya Sheikh. I thought about the rights of my wife and I have not divorced her. I do not deserve such a beating."

Still struggling, the Sheikh declares, "Ever since the day you came to me, I cannot cusp my hands in prayer without seeing your wife's pussy.'"

'You know, sister,' Kameena asked, pointing to her shoe

'Yes, Kameena.'

'Your shoe is really lovely.'

'Shall I take it off, eh, you hoodlum, and let you know how it feels next to your skin?' Khairaan replied.

'Good job I didn't say I like your dress.'

Khairaan whacked him, looked across at the women and said, 'This Imam goes for a walk with his wife. They walk past some animals. All the animals are fucking. The wife gets horny and asks, "How does the male know it is time to do this thing?"

"He can smell the scent of the female."

"Why do you always have a cold?" she asks.'

Kameena retorts, 'That night, the same Imam went home to his own wife and as per his habit after Isha prayers, the evening prayers, he picked up a book, went to bed with his wife and started reading, and after a little while his wife asks, "I see your cold has cleared."

"No, it is still there."

"Then why do you keep putting your finger in my crutch?"

"It helps to turn the pages," the Imam replies.'

'As I was saying, sister Khairaan,' interjects Kanjar, 'this Imam and his best friend's wife start having an affair. Usually, as soon as his best friend leaves for work, the Imam turns up and jumps into bed with his wife. One day, the friend forgets something and goes back home and sees his wife and the Imam at it. The friend is enraged. The wife quickly puts her clothes on and runs behind her husband, and points to the Imam, saying, "Go on husband. Beat that bastard. Doesn't he realise he is your best friend."

The Imam gets really irate at this. He gets dressed. He is a huge man. He rolls up his sleeves and picks up an axe.

The wife runs behind the Imam and points to her husband, saying, "Go on, kill that bastard husband of mine. He can't do it himself and won't let anyone else do it either."'

'A mother is asleep with her daughter and son on the roof of their house in the village.' Khairaan said. 'It is the middle of a moonlit night. The animals are also asleep. The mother is disturbed by something, sits up in bed and asks, "Daughter, daughter, what was that noise?"

The daughter wakes up, looks around and replies, "I can see three men coming down the hill, mother. They are coming towards our house."

"They could be bandits, daughter,' the mother says. 'Quickly, hide yourself, we must protect your honour. These are bad times."

"One of them has a beard, mother."

"Hurry, daughter, hide your brother, we must protect his honour as well. These are bad times."

"Oh mother, one of them is a fauji, a soldier."

"May Allah save us, daughter," the mother says. "Hide the kata, the male buffalo, as well. These are bad times.'"

'One night, bandits are stealing a poor man's buffaloes,' Kameena said. 'He wakes up and fights the thieves. They strip him naked, tie him upside down from a tree and steal his animals. In the morning, when the villagers free him, the man does not get dressed but picks up a stick and starts beating a baby buffalo which the thieves missed. The villagers ask him, "Why are you beating this poor creature, he is all you have left."

"As I was hanging upside down from the tree all night," the poor man replied, 'this little bastard thought I was his mother.'"

All of a sudden, there is an uncomfortable silence as Kanjar and Kameena walk off and go towards their respective masters. After a short consultation, they come back and are joined by Lither and Khairaan, and the four of them whisper to each other, and then Lither turns to the Jirga and says, 'It is time for you to pronounce your judgement.'

Kanjar raises his hands skywards, then bows to the

Jirga and says, 'As God is my witness, this Kanjar has, in his humblest opinion, won the white woman for *his* master.'

'And I trust the justice of our esteemed Jirga,' Kameena said, after bowing respectfully, 'and I pray that I have won the white woman for *my* master; and on his behalf, I would like to state that he also wants the white man, and is prepared to share him.'

'Though I entered the competition unprepared,' Khairaan said to the Jirga, 'even so, I added quality and wisdom, more than this Kanjar and this Kameena. Therefore, I trust you will give me the white woman and the white man.'

I was beginning to fume with anger, thinking our lives cannot be decided on the basis of who told the best filthy jokes, no matter how good or subversive they may have been. I looked across at Tipsy. She was trembling, her face in her hands.

I stood up and shouted, 'No one is taking my friend, and no one is having my arse without my consent. I demand a fair chance.'

'Give him a chance,' a woman shouted.

Then others, both men and women, joined in, demanding I be given a chance.

I could see everyone in the Jirga nodding in agreement. Lither went over to the two men in black, and came back a moment later and pronounced, 'The white man can defend himself.'

'But make sure he really is a man, first,' a woman shouted out.

Khairaan whispered something to Kanjar and Kameena, who ran off, and she waved at me to come forward. I did, a little unsure of what I was getting myself into.

Kanjar and Kameena returned, carrying some cloth in their hands. With the help of Lither, they spread the cloth out and formed a circle around me and Khairaan. With my private parts out of view, Khairaan frisked me all over. First my torso and arms, then each leg in turn, and then grabbed my penis and started playing with it with her hand. I began to get erect. She stopped, walked away from me and said to the crowd, 'He is certainly a man.'

'How much of one?' a woman asked.

The cloth was taken away and I felt utterly humiliated, standing there in the condition I found myself in, but I was grateful that Khairaan had not answered the last question.

Part III: White Man Fights for His Arse

'So you think you white men can beat us at our own game?' Khairaan asked as soon as she saw me.

'I will certainly try,' I replied.

'You're English,' Khairaan laughed, 'You'll never win.'

'We won the world cup in 1966,' I replied flippantly, but regretted the words as soon as they stumbled out of my mouth.

'The only game that matters out here is cricket,' she said as she struck me across my back with her slap-paddle. I was not expecting her to do this. It made a loud noise, but, strangely, it did not hurt as much as one would think, and I instinctively let out an 'Ahh.'

It was not an *ahh* of pain, but more of one filled with sexual arousal, something that Khairaan picked up on almost immediately.

'English man likes this, eh?' she asked in a hushed voice, and then hit me again.

This really is not the time for you to go off on your sexual fantasies, Frank, I thought, but still couldn't help smiling back at Khairaan for her sharp observation.

Before standing up to tell stories, I had made a mental note of some of those I remembered from our database of such material: Iranian ones, Palestinian, American, German and Pakistani, and set out to present these, saying calmly and loudly, 'So, this Ayatollah is in an aeroplane sitting next to a young woman. The woman is reading a document. Each page has an image of a penis on it. The Ayatollah begins to get aroused.

So, he is on the aeroplane with this young lady, and she is reading this big book and looking at all these pictures of penises, and he starts a conversation with her, "Young lady, may I ask you where you are travelling to?"

"Sir, this plane flies from London to Tehran only," she snaps back at him, "where do you think I am going to?"

"Oh, I see," he replies. "Do you mind telling me why you were in London?"

"I came to do my PhD," she replies, "to get a doctorate."

"Do you mind if I ask you what you are reading?"

"I am revising my PhD thesis, sir."

"Mahashahalla, we need more PhDs in Iran to defeat the Great Satan,' and then the Ayatollah says, "May I ask why there is a picture of a penis on every page?"

"I studied penises, sir."

"Did you have to conduct a lot of field research?"

"Oh yes, sir, lots and lots," she replies, "and lots."

"Subhanallah, Allah is perfect,' he says. "May I know what conclusions you came to?'

"The longest are Italian," she replies, "but the hardest were Iranian."

"Jazak Allah Khair, may the almighty reward you with blessings for such a discovery," he says, and then asks, "What is your name young lady?"

"First, could you please tell me your name sir?"

"My name is Antonio Rafsanjani," he replies.'

Khairaan looks a bit bewildered, and I look across at the audience. Not a single smile.

'Well, I think we have had enough of Mullahs and Lullahs, and dicks,' Khairaan said.

'So, Alpha sperm, the lead sperm, is leading the

charge,' I said. 'All the other sperms are following him. Suddenly, Alpha sperm comes to a stop. He turns around, raises his hand in front of all the other sperms and says, "Brothers, stop! Wrong hole!"'

'You are obsessed with holes,' Khairaan said, hitting me.

'He's a man, isn't he?' a woman shouted.

Before Khairaan could reply, I said, 'So, American President Donald Trump and the Pope both die on the same day. Their papers get mixed up, and Trump ends up going to heaven and the Pope to hell. At the gates of hell, the Pope protests, maintaining that he has never committed a sin and is therefore entitled to go to heaven, and surely there must have been a mistake. An investigation is launched, and finally the mess is sorted out. The Pope is overjoyed at being sent up to heaven. Trump is kicked out of heaven and sent down to hell.

So, the Pope is going up to heaven as Trump is coming down. The two men meet half way. The Pope waves across to Trump and asks, 'Did you meet the Virgin Mary?'

"Oops," Trump replies.'

I expected Khairaan to laugh, or at least smile, but all she had was a puzzled look.

It suddenly occurred to me that no one could understand what I had just said as the idea of the Virgin Mary does not exist among Muslims. Certainly, if the look on Khairaan's face was anything to go by, I was definitely not heading for any victory. So I quickly changed the subject and said, 'So President Obama walks into a school in America and tells the children they can ask him anything, and today he will tell the truth. A child raises his hand and asks, "My father says you listen to everyone's conversations."

"He is not your father," President Obama replies.'

You did that well, Frank, I thought. Not a single giggle. Maybe you should have explained much more about the setting of the story, about Big Brother America, and all the electronic monitoring.

Khairaan frowned and whacked me across the back. At least she understood this one, I thought. She hit me again, saying, 'This man with an enormous dick fucks his wife. She complains about his dick reaching her kidneys and hurting her. She goes to see the doctor to see what can be done. The doctor says, "This is a minor medical matter. We can cut his dick."

"No, no, no!" the woman protests. "Isn't it possible to move my kidneys out of the way?"

'She must have had more pricks in her than a second hand dartboard,' I laughed, but went quiet from the look that Khairaan gave back. Of course, I thought, who on earth would know what a dartboard is out here?

Come on, Frank, I thought, you can do better, and then I remembered a story and said, 'So, Egypt's President Nasser dies. All the generals, top Sheikhs and politicians gather to decide where to bury him, such a famous man.

The Prime Minister suggests he be buried in the grave of the Unknown Soldier, but the generals protest, saying, "He was not unknown and no longer a soldier." And one of them suggests, "One as famous as our late leader should be buried in Giza."

The Sheikhs protest at this suggestion, "For our beloved leader, a leader of the Ummah, to be buried among the Pagans would be an insult to the Muslim world."

Eventually, a cleaner suggests, "A person as important as our President Nasser can only be buried in the Holy Land, in Palestine."

Everyone stands up and protests in unison, "The last time an important person was buried there, he came back to life three days later.'"

I looked around. Silence. I need to change my strategy, I think, these people are perhaps only interested in religious types of stories.

As Khairaan raises the slap-paddle to strike me, I ask her, 'Do you know who Adolf Hitler was?'

Khairaan whacks me, asking, 'Was he that horrible little German white man who fought that horrible big fat English white man and killed us for fun along the way?'

'So Hitler knocks on the door of heaven. Jesus opens it. Hitler wants to get in, but Jesus stops him and asks, "Where is your visa?"

"Don't have it, mate. Lost everything during the bombing raids"

"What is your name?" Jesus asks

"Adolf Leon Hitler."

Jesus looks through his records, shakes his head and says, "Sorry, there is no Adolf Leon Hitler."

"Well of course there wouldn't be,' Adolf Hitler says, "My father didn't actually register the Leon bit. He just baptised me as Adolf Hitler."

Jesus looks over his list again and says, "Sorry, you must go to hell, your name is not on this list.

"Oh fuck, Jesus…"

"No bad language allowed at the gate of heaven," Jesus interrupts

"Sorry, Jesus, there must be a mistake."

"Dad does not make mistakes," Jesus says.

"Alright then, Jesus Christ, I'll make you an offer you can't refuse."

"Go on, what?"

"I will give you six million Deutschmarks. You will be able to buy anything you like in Germany."

"OK, let me go ask my dad."

Jesus goes before God.

"Dad, will you please make an exception and let a man into heaven whose name is not on the list?"

"What is his name?" God asks.

"Adolf Hitler."

"He killed millions of people, including six million Jews in Europe. Tell him to fuck off."

Jesus comes back to Hitler and says, "My dad says fuck off!"

"OK, I'll tell you what. Not only will I give you six

million Deutschmarks, I will also give you Germany's highest medal, the Iron Cross. Not only will you be able to buy anything you like, but you will also be the most respected person in the country."

"OK, let me ask my dad again."

Jesus goes back in front of God and pleads, "Dad, please let him in. He will not only give me six million Deutschmarks but also the medal of highest honour, the Iron Cross. I will be the most respected man in Germany."

God gets angry with Jesus and asks, "How are you going to carry the Iron Cross, when you couldn't even carry the fucking wooden one?"'

All of a sudden there is great excitement in the crowd. I feel a sense of pride rush through me at having worked out that people in this part of the world have a simple and well understandable social make up. They like religious type stories, I think, like the one I've just told. But I am completely wrong. Everyone is looking past me at Tipsy. She was walking towards me. A couple of women grabbed her and tried to force her to sit again, but she struggled to break free of them. Three armed men were rushing towards her, when Khairaan shouted, 'No one will touch her until the competition is over.'

Men and women shouted in agreement with Khairaan. The armed men stopped and looked back towards the elders, one of whom stood up and shook his head. The armed men stepped back and Tipsy walked past them.

'This ridiculous competition has gone far enough,' Tipsy shouted at Khairaan.

Tipsy looked quite magnificent dressed in her bridal clothes, and walked with such grace, almost as if she was walking on air. When she got close to us, she said. 'I demand the right to defend myself as well.'

'We don't get brides to catch thieves,' Khairaan said.

'I am not a bride but a captive,' Tipsy said, 'and I can do as well as any man here.'

Khairaan nodded, and went and talked to the elders. As she did this, Tipsy said to me, 'The way you are going, not only will you have me carried away by one of these bearded things, but they will also have your arse as well. And,' she added, 'you won't just be his bitch.'

'I thought I told the last story rather well,' I replied.

'You are utterly dull. Monotonous. Words fall out of your mouth like bricks, and you are so out of touch with the local culture. The last one you told could have got you killed. It was bordering on blasphemous, and that is punishable by death in this country. And besides, you are not in Birmingham giving a lecture to students,' Tipsy paused and then added, 'Your tone is so flat, so boring, I'm surprised none of them has killed you so far.'

I found her words quite offensive, but given the delicacy of our situation, I pursed my lips and asked her calmly, 'How many stories do you remember?'

'Enough,' she replied, and then mocked, 'All that *subversive* shite you kept sending me might have some use now.'

Khairaan came back from talking to the elders and hit Tipsy with her slap-paddle, saying, 'So be it.'

'Why do men have a hole in their dick?' Tipsy asked Khairaan.

'To piss!' Khairaan replied

'No, it is so that oxygen can get to their brains.'

Tipsy waited for a moment and then said, 'There was once a famous King. A very powerful King, who liked getting buggered by young boys.'

'Was he a Pakistani King?' Khairaan asked.

'No,' Tipsy replied, 'There was no Pakistan then. He was definitely English, as you will understand when I finish my story.'

Dear God, I thought, what have we got ourselves into?

Tipsy looked so self-confident, and talked without a hint of fear in her voice as she continued, 'In order to protect his secret, the King has the boys executed, after fucking them. One day a new boy is brought for the King. But this boy also likes getting buggered. The boy is sent into the King's bedroom. When the King enters the bedroom, the new boy is undressed and bent over. The King doesn't notice this, gets undressed and also bends over.

"You do it Sire," the boy says.

"No, you must do it," the King insists.

"But, please, you must at least go first, Sire."

The King gets dressed and calls his security. The guard turns up, sword in hand, ready to execute the boy.

"Take this boy and give him whatever he asks for," the King orders the guard.

"But, your Majesty, I have always beheaded the boys afterwards. Why make an exception of him?"

And the King replies, "He has royal taste. He is also a potential King. "'

I was really taken aback by the manner of Tipsy telling her story, but also by the way it was received.

'God has made all of you intelligent people,' Tipsy said, waving a hand across the audience from the women to the men. 'You must all remember Prime Minister Tony Blair and President Bush.' She paused, and I saw Khairaan and many others nodding. Tipsy continued, 'In 2005, they both meet in Gleneagles, Scotland. They decide to go for a quiet walk, just the two of them. There are lots of sheep in the fields where they walk. The sheep run away in terror as they see the two of them coming towards them. President Bush notices a sheep with its head stuck in a fence and tells the Secret Servicemen who are following them to go away. They do.

Bush steps towards the sheep. It tries hard to pull its head out of the hole into which it's stuck. The more it tries, the more it wiggles its arse, and the more it does this, the hornier President Bush gets.

So Bush unzips himself, and fucks the sheep. He fucks it and fucks it until finally he comes, and then turns around to Blair and says, "Tony, your turn."

Blair leans forward, bends down and then stands up again, replying "Sorry, sir, I can't get my head through that hole."'

Tipsy launched straight into the next story, walking in front of her audience, with the confidence of a professional performer. She stopped in front of the women and said, 'You know how it is, girls, as they say in Arabic, "The dick of a stranger is always sweeter." Anyway, this man has cancer. He has a few days left. His wife goes to the doctor with him. The doctor calls her in on her own and says, "I have good news for you. Your husband's cancer can be cured." He gives her some pills and says, "Give him one of these tablets an hour before he goes to bed. He will get a massive hard-on. And you must fuck him every day, as much as he can manage. This will release chemicals in his brain which will kill the cancer."

When she comes out, her husband asks, "What did the doctor say?"

"Nothing can be done for you."'

Khairaan comes up to me as Tipsy finishes and hits me across the back, saying, "Does the woman have to save your arse, or are you going to say something?'

My mind went blank. Perhaps I was feeling over-awed, but before I could say anything, Khairaan said, 'This villager goes out to buy a manji, a bed. After a lot of haggling, he gets the price reduced to 500 rupees. He picks the manji up, puts it on his head and sets off proudly homewards. Along the way, he meets a number of friends.

"How much did you buy that for?" the first friend asks.

"500 rupees," replies the villager.

"You simple motherfucker, you got buggered. I could have bought it for 300," the friend says.

The villager shrugs his shoulders and walks on. He meets another friend.

"How much did you buy that for?" the friend asks.

"300," the villager replies.

"You simple motherfucker, you really got buggered. I could have got it for 200 rupees," the second friend says.

The villager shrugs his shoulders and walks on and meets another friend, who asks, "How much did you buy that for?"

The villager thinks for a while and replies: "100 rupees."

"You simple motherfucker, you really got buggered. I could have got it for 50," the friend says.

The villager gets very upset, and smashes the manji to bits. He then thinks he might as well take it home and use it as firewood. He picks up the pieces, rolls them up, puts them on top of his head and walks on homewards. A short while later he meets his dad.

"What have you been doing all day?" his father asks.

"Getting buggered," the villager replies

"Did you have to take a manji with you?" the father asks.'

I was trying to work out what to say when Khairaan launched into another story, 'A father finds out that his son is feeling randy again and is about to fuck a girl from their village, and gives his son some money, saying, "Son, take this money and go to the city and fuck a prostitute. In our village all the women are like your mother and sister, we must preserve the honour and status of the village."

The son takes the money and sets off to the city. As he is leaving the house, he meets his sister, who notices he has money in his pocket and says, "Where have you got the money from brother, and where are you going to?"

"Father gave me the money so that I can go fuck a prostitute in the city," the brother replies

"I don't have any money, and could really do with some. Why don't you do it with me, brother?"

"How can you suggest such a thing, sister?"

"It's only a bit of flesh against flesh. You won't last long, and it's a shame to waste all this money for just a few minutes," she says.

The brother thinks about it and agrees with his sister not to waste the money. He gives her the money and puts his dick inside her, and says, "Your pussy is so big?"

"That's what dad says," she replies, and then adds, "your dick is so long."

'"That's what mum says," he replies.'

As Khairaan was talking, Tipsy came closer to me and quickly whispered, 'Say something. If not for you, then for me.'

'So, an angel is walking around trying to sell brains of famous leaders,' I said. 'He is calling out, "Brains, buy famous brains: General Zia, 100; Caliph Al Baghdadi, 2000; Prime Minster Tony Blair, 5000; President Trump, 1 million."

A man asks the angel, "So was Trump a genius?"

"No, it has never been used," the angel replies.'

'You can't just throw anything in, this is a very serious competition,' Tipsy snapped at me before starting her next story.

'Didn't you say you were from Jordan?' Tipsy asked Khairiaan.

'No, I said I lived in Lebanon,' Khairaan replied.

'Do you know what they say in Jordan about the Lebanese?' Tipsy asked.

Khairaan whacked me across my back and said to Tipsy, 'Get on with it.'

I didn't ask Khairaan why the hell she had hit me when she wanted Tipsy to do something!

'This old married couple is sitting around,' Tipsy said, 'and the husband says to his wife, "Have you ever been unfaithful to me? You can tell me now, it doesn't matter. We are old now."

"Yes, three times," the wife replies.

"When was the first time?" the husband asks.

"Do you remember when you wanted a bank loan, but the manager refused."

"Yes."

"Why do you think you got it?"

Oh, Abu Khalil, that bastard, the husband thinks, I thought he was a good pious man. But he died a long time ago. It doesn't matter now. And then the husband asks, "When was the second time?"

"Do you remember how your manager refused your promotion?" the wife replies.
"Yes."

"Why do you think he changed his mind?"
Oh George, that bastard, the husband thinks, and I thought he was my best friend. But he has gone to Kuwait now. It doesn't matter now.

"When was the next time?" the husband asks.
"Do you remember when you stood in the elections for Mayor of the village?"
"Yes."

"Do you remember you were short of 70 votes for victory in the first round?'"
I said, stepping in between Tipsy and Khairaan, 'So, you know, Tipsy, this first old man asks the second old man, "Do you remember when we were young and we chased young women?"

"Yes, I do, but can you remind me why we did that," the second old man replies.'

Khairaan ignored me and replied to Tipsy, 'My husband is so rude about me sometimes. My son has a bad habit, he can't resist brothels, and my husband tries to dissuade him from going to brothels, and finds my son a pretty bride and says, "Son, I have found you a very pretty wife, now you have to stop going to brothels."

"Why is that dad?"

"If you keep going to brothels, you will catch an illness."

"Is that so dad?"

"If you catch the illness, then she will catch the illness."

"Is that so dad?"

"Yes, and if she catches the illness, then I will catch the illness."

"Is that so dad?"

"Yes, and if I catch the illness, then your mother will catch the illness."

"Is that so dad?"

"Yes, and If your mother catches the illness, then the whole village will catch it.'"

Tipsy is about to open her mouth when I say, 'So, there were these two servants trying to work out what sex was about. The first servant asks, "Is sex labour or fun?"

"I am sure it is fun," the second servant replies, "If it was labour, then the Master would ask us to do it.'"

Once again Khairaan ignored me and said, 'You know, Miss Tipsy, in my village we have a tradition where the Khala, the aunty, takes the groom and shows him what to do. It is the wedding night and the guests have all gone to bed. So, Khala goes to the bride, and asks her if she would like to go to bed. The bride is eager and quickly gets undressed and jumps into bed.

The Aunty goes up to the groom and says, "OK son, come along. It's time."

The groom follows the aunty to the bride's room. She stops outside the room and tells the groom, "Drop your pants."

He does as he is ordered. The Aunty rubs her hand up and down his thighs until he gets a hard on. Once he is fully erect, the aunty grabs his dick, leads him into the brides room and asks the bride, "Daughter, are you ready to receive your husband's dick."

"I am aunty."

"Open your legs, then," says the aunty.

The bride opens her legs and the aunty pulls the groom towards her bed. When she gets to the bed, the aunty places the tip of the dick on the pussy of the bride and asks, "Do you want to take it in?"

"Yes, aunty," the bride replies.

And the aunty puts one hand on the arse of the

groom and pushes some dick in, and then asks the bride, "Daughter, do you want some more?"

"Yes please, Aunty."

The Aunty carefully pushes some more dick into the bride and asks, "Daughter, do you want some more?"

"Yes, oh yes please, aunty."

The aunty pushes some more dick into the bride.

Then the bride says, "More please, aunty, more!"

The aunty raises her hands in front of the bride and says, "That's all that is written in your kismet, your fate, daughter."

The bride gets angry and shouts at the aunty, "Father was right, there is no barakat, blessings, in your hand.'"

Tipsy came close to me and whispered, 'Religious ones.'

I just blurted out, 'So, I know lots of suicide bombings have been taking place here in Pakistan and it has been getting more and more difficult to find new volunteer bombers. So, there is this depressed American. He wants to end his life and phones the Samaritans, and is transferred to a call centre in Pakistan. The

American says, "I am so fed up with my life. I've lost my job, my house has been repossessed, my wife has left me. The financial system is in free fall. The cops are on a killing spree. Trump has been elected. I can't see the purpose of living and just want to die."

The Pakistani counsellor asks, "Can you drive a truck?"'

I went straight into the next few stories, one after the other, 'So, this Jihadi blows himself to smithereens and wakes up in heaven, where he is welcomed by an angel who greets him, "Welcome to Heaven."

"Am I really in Heaven?" the Jihadi asks.

"Yes. That's the good news for you," the angel replies. "What is your wish?"

"70 hoors, please!" the Jihadi asks.

"Yes, indeed, you may have them," and just like that, 70 hoors materialize. However, the angel says, "But I have some bad news for you. Your testicles were left behind when you were blown to smithereens."'

'So, I have this cartoon from a newspaper in my office. There is a class of Jihadis. The teacher is standing at the front wearing a suicide belt. He says, "Now class. Pay attention. I can only demonstrate this once.'"

Tipsy and Khairaan exchanged a look that I thought was a bit too intimate. Given our lives were at stake, I didn't stop for long, and told four stories quickly.

'So, a Pakistani goes to the United States of America. He sees an old lady with a dog. The dog frees itself and runs onto a busy road. The old lady runs after her dog. She is about to be hit by a car. The Pakistani dives and saves the old lady. The dog is run over by the car and killed. A journalist happens to be passing, takes out his notebook and quickly jots down a head-line: *Local Hero Saves Lady*.

The Pakistan sees what the journalist has written down and says to him, "I am not a local."

So, the journalist changes the headline: *Foreign Hero Saves Lady*

"Actually I am a Pakistani," the Pakistani says.

So, the journalist changes the heading to: *Terrorist Kills Dog.*'

'So, King Hussain of Jordan issues a new postage

stamp with his picture on it. People start demonstrating against the new stamp. King Hussain goes outside dressed as an ordinary person and asks a demonstrator, "Why are you protesting against this new stamp?"

"Like everything else in Jordon, it does not work."

King Hussain examines the stamp and says, "Look, this is perfect."

"It does not stick," the demonstrator replies.

King Hussain licks the stamp and sticks it onto a piece of paper.

"Oh dear, we have been spitting on the wrong side."

'So, President Arafat gives a speech on the radio, "Colonisers always fuck the colonised, just like Israelis fucked us, and then they too get fucked. So, let us fuck them out of existence. I order you to produce a Palestinian baby. It is like killing an Israeli.'

A husband and wife are listening to President Arafat, and the wife asks, "So shall we kill an Israeli tonight?"

"Yes," the husband replies.

They fuck all night, and the next day, the wife says, "Shall we kill another Israeli tonight?"

"If you like," the husband replies.

They fuck all night, and the next day the wife says, "I really need to kill an Israeli tonight?"

"Do we have to?" the husband replies, "I am knackered."

"Yes," the wife says, "it is our national duty."

They fuck all night and the next day the wife says, "Today is Jumma al Mubarak, Blessed Friday. We have to kill an Israeli tonight."

"I can't liberate Palestine on my own!" the husband snaps.'"

'So, this Palestinian man goes up to the Palestinian leader, Yasar Arafat, and asks, "President Arafat, why don't you spend more time with your wife?"

"Because I am married to the cause," Arafat replies.

"Do you have to fuck it every day, then?" the man asks.'

I looked around. Judging by the fidgeting crowd, I might have been on a streak, but it clearly did not look like it was a winning streak. Come on, Frank, think, I thought. Even if you are getting tired, maybe, maybe they don't understand things in far off lands; maybe you should tell them local stories.

The air began to fill with the scent of roasting

meat, and I felt hunger rumbling in my stomach, but I continued.

'So, as you know, Pakistan and India are always in competition with each other. Pakistan, understandably, has an inferiority complex. You know, when India detonated a nuclear device in Indian Gujarat, Pakistan responded by detonating two nuclear bombs in Pakistani Balouchistan.

So, this cow milking competition takes place in Lahore. And you Pakistanis are only concerned with beating India, yes. Hundreds of people form circles around the competing cows. Drums start beating. Lahoris dance and dance.

First comes the American cow. It gives 30 kilos of milk, and as you Pakistanis call litres '*kilos*', so will I. And the drums beat louder, and the Lahoris dance. The crowd cheers. Then it is the turn of the French. It gives 20 kilos. The German one follows, and it gives 15 kilos. Each time the crowd celebrates. There are only two cows left. The Indian and Pakistani.

The Indian cow is a well-polished Nagori breed, versus Pakistan's brown-skinned emaciated Sahiwali. To the utter jubilation of the crowd, the Indian cow gives only 3 kilos.

But the Pakistan milkman manages to get only 1

kilo from his, which he raises triumphantly in front of the crowd. Everyone goes wild with anger and starts to beat the milkman.

"Brothers, stop, don't beat me!" he begs. "Can't you see mine is a bull?"'

Just as I finished, Khairaan clapped her hands and shouted, 'Enough! Let the judgement begin.'

She turned to Tipsy and me, and said, 'You must go to the tent in the cave whilst the Jirga decides.

A couple of armed men dressed in black came up behind Khairaan.

'Move,' she said coldly.

'I turned around and Tipsy was being led by her guards into the mouth of the cave, which I had not realised was the darkness behind her when I first saw her.

Small re-chargeable battery-operated torches lit up a footpath that snaked into the cave. I followed Tipsy and her guards, and mine followed me. When we had gone a short distance inside, we walked into a beautiful cool gust of wind. I looked up and could see small cracks, with streaks of moonlight. Along the sides of the cave were holes of every shape and size; some large, with round openings, which could have been carved, and which like the footpath had torches placed in front of them; others were small dark patches ,and some with sharp blade-like fronts. We stopped in front of a huge tent, and judging by the way Tipsy walked up to it and unzipped it, she had been here before. The guards stopped and I followed Tipsy into the tent. It was luxuriously furnished, with carpets, cushions, and a coffee table with a box of tissues, flowers, all manner of fruit in a large ceramic bowl and mineral water bottles.

'Did you tell the Embassy you were coming here?' Tipsy asked, looking at the shadows of the guards who had stopped outside the entrance of the tent.

'No,' I said.

'Why not?'

'You asked me not to.'

Tipsy rushed towards me, hugged me and cried.

The tent flap opened, and one of the female guards walked in, prodded me in the back with the barrel of her Kalashnikov and said, 'This is not allowed.'

I too had started to cry, and ignored the guard. She unclipped the safety and said, 'No hugging.'

Tipsy pulled away. The guard picked up the box of tissues and offered it to Tipsy, who took one and wiped her tears, and then the guard did the same to me, and I also took one and did the same.

After the guard left, I commented to Tipsy, 'All this doesn't feel real.'

'It's very real,' Tipsy answered, sitting down on the floor in front of the coffee table and leaning back against a large round cushion. After a little while, a guard came inside. He was followed by two men carrying trays of food and drink in their hands. The tent quickly filled with the scent of roasted meat and freshly baked naans.

The men placed the food trays on the coffee table and one of them poured a milky drink into two glasses, offering one to me and the other to Tipsy. We were both thirsty and immediately started drinking. The cold drink was delicious. It was a lassi, I thought, I had often had it, but in this one I could taste almonds, sugar and a whole host of other flavours.

As we were drinking, we were left alone again. I opened a bottle of water and washed my hands, and offered some water to Tipsy, who ignored me as she was already eating. We ate and drank a few more glasses of the lassi in silence. After eating my fill, I stood up and asked Tipsy, as I walked to the furthest end of the tent, 'Is there a back way out of this cave?'

As I was about to touch the side of the tent, she shouted, 'Stop!'

I looked back towards her. She was up on her knees.

'Move back from that end,' she said quickly.

I turned around and saw the shadow of a snake, a King Cobra, its crown fully open on the other side of the tent. It hissed and struck the tent as I jumped back.

'They are everywhere in the cave,' Tipsy said. And then she laughed, 'Don't worry, their fangs can't get through the canvas.'

'We really are beyond the back of beyond,' I said, 'wherever beyond might be.'

'We are not,' Tipsy answered.

'Do you know where we are?'

'No,' she replied, 'but they are really high-tech. They know pretty much everything about us. About our university. Especially about your work on collecting dirty stories and proverbial filth from Pakistan and around the world. About how you believe that such tales resist religious and dictatorial traditions and institutions by stripping them down into humour. And it was *they* who sent the video link to you.'

'Did you find the Holy Man?' I asked.

Tipsy inhaled deeply and replied, 'He was brought to meet me in this very tent, with Khairaan. He looked as if he hadn't aged, but his mind was gone. It was obvious he had dementia.'

'So, is he your father?'

'If he is my father, then the man that fathered me was lost somewhere back in history.'

For fuck's sake, I thought, here we are about to be auctioned off to some of the strangest Muslims in the world, and you are faffing on about some philosophical shite, but said, 'Tipsy, I don't think what we just drank was lassi,' while finishing off the last of it. 'I think I am high as a kite and am beginning to hallucinate.'

'It wasn't lassi,' Tipsy laughed. 'It was Bhang, that's what they call it, and I am tripping too.'

'It was Bhang,' I laughed, feeling lightheaded. 'I thought I could taste cannabis in it.'

'So could I,' Tipsy said, moving her head to the rhythm of the music, which was now much louder than before.

'So is he your bloody father or not?'

'Khairaan said something, but I just can't remember it, you know.'

'I know,' I said, placing my head in Tipsy's lap. She started to run her fingers though my hair. I closed my eyes and listened to men and women laughing outside the tent.

'Frank,' Tipsy said in the voice of a sexy goddess.

'Yes, goddess Tipsy,' I replied.

'I don't know why anyone on this earth, or anywhere in the universe, would want your arse.'

'Don't you, goddess?' I asked. 'It only wobbles a bit!'

My goddess didn't answer, but closed her eyes and fell asleep. I too closed my eyes and drifted off somewhere above in the psychedelic universe, and said, 'If I win and you lose, I will give you my victory. They can have my arse.'

'That's the most romantic thing anyone has ever said to me,' Tipsy said sleepily.

I was confused.

'You said you would give your arse to this lot to save me,' Tipsy said.

Tipsy leaned down, kissed me on the lips and put her tongue in my mouth. My dick rose to the occasion. Tipsy lifted her dress, and I helped her take off her knickers. Just then, Khairaan burst into the tent. I was expecting her to snatch Tipsy off me, but instead she held her hand out to me and said, 'Take this!'

It was a condom.

'Safe sex please, we are Pakistanis,' Khairaan said and left.

There was laughter, shouting, drumming and

singing outside. Tipsy stood up and both of us stepped towards the entrance to the tent. Tipsy popped her head outside and whispered to me, 'There's no guard.'

I popped my head out as well, and what I saw was a scene befitting the temples of Khajuraho. Everyone was fucking each other. It was an orgy.

To my horror, Tipsy walked out, laughing, and went up to the Irishman, who was playing with his dick. He turned his back to me as Tipsy got closer. I was petrified lest someone grab her, but no one touched her and she came back a few moments later.

'What did you do?' I asked.

'I don't know,' she replied, 'it was instinctive.'

'What was?' I asked.

We both laughed a stoned laugh, looked at each other for a bit, then went back into the tent. I bit open the condom, slipped it on and we fucked for a couple of centuries and then fell into a deep sleep in each other's embrace.

Some time later, Tipsy pressed on my chin and woke me up, saying, 'We must find a way out of here.'

I felt horny again and stroked her leg, saying, 'Why?' I wanted to at least get another shag in before whatever fate came our way.

'Escape,' she replied, slapping my hand.

'They'll kill us if we try,' I said.

'Shh,' Tipsy said, standing up. 'Why is it so quiet outside?'

It was indeed strangely silent, and I said, 'Maybe they are all praying.'

We waited for a few moments in apprehensive silence until Tipsy said, 'We can't stay here all day.'

There was a smell of burning plastic in the air outside the tent. I stepped cautiously towards the mouth of the cave. Tipsy was behind me. Apart from discarded rubbish, there was no one around. The smell was coming from a small pit. A few unburned condoms were sitting among a hoard of burnt ones. I turned around, but could not see Tipsy.

Stepping down from the edge of the cave, I called out for Tipsy. I ran back into the cave and called out to her, but only the echo of my voice came as a reply. I ran out and ran down the path that led out of the mouth of the cave and, after a turn, I saw her standing in the middle of the path. She was looking straight at me.

'There is no one but us here,' she said.

'Where did they all go?' I asked.

She put her arm in mine and I realised she was

limping. I looked down, and she was bleeding from the ankles.

'It's nothing serious.'

'Shall I carry you?' I asked.

She smiled.

I gave her a piggyback and we set off down the dirt road. We had only gone a few yards when I slipped and Tipsy got her dress caught in a thorn bush. She pulled it free violently, and tore it in many places.

'How far do we have to go do you think?' she asked.

'Until we get there,' I replied.

We went down the road for an hour or so, stopping for rests every few minutes. Eventually, I saw a car with a man standing beside it. He saw us before we had a chance to hide. He came running towards us and said, in English, 'Mister Frank, sir! My name is Pakka Khan Halwaee, or PKH to my friends. I have been waiting here for five hours now,' he said, moving his head from right to left, 'and English brides run away as well, no?'

'Who sent you?' I asked, wondering where I had come across PKH.

Tipsy got off my back, and gave me a quizzical look.

'The company,' he replied, stepping towards me

with an envelope in his hand. 'I was told to give you this, pick you up, and drop you off.'

The driver was around ten years older than me.

Tipsy took the envelope from him and opened it. It had our passports in it and a note. She read the note and showed it to me. It said: *Leave Pakistan.*

We got into the taxi and as the vehicle moved off, I said, 'Can you please take me to my hotel …'

I was about to tell him which one, when he interrupted me and said, 'I am booked to drop you at Islamabad airport, sir,' he paused, and then added, 'You two are the first people I have ever heard of to come out from the mela of here.'

We sat silently for a while as the car went along the dirt road. I was a bit relieved, in that at least he had heard of what went on here.

'Who are the people who have this festival here?' I asked as we drove past a lone house at the edge of a village.

'Don't know, sir,' he replied, giving me a suspicious look in his mirror. 'They are very powerful, and many are very rich. I have heard they have a strange festival once a year, but they move it from place to place, and when they do have it, they have armed guards all around it. Not even sparrows can get in and out.' Then his voice took on a serious tone, 'You must leave. Foreigners not safe in Pakistan outside the Blue Area in Islamabad.'

'What's happened?' I asked.

'Someone has broken into General Zia's grave and stolen him,' the driver said. 'They say the thieves are two foreign professors.'

Tipsy ignored the driver and said to me, 'You know, mother used to say father had a heart-shaped birth mark on his dick.'

The last thing I wanted to hear was anything else to do with her father, and I snapped, 'Go on, tell me, on his dick?'

'I hear you speak our language really good, sir?' the driver asked me.

'I can get by without any problems,' I replied, switching to Pothohari.

'Does Madam speak my language?' he asked.

Tipsy dug her nails into my arm and I understood what this meant, and replied, 'No, nothing.'

'I have a heart-shaped birth mark on my dick,' the driver boasted in Pothohari, 'with my full name, in English, PAKKA KHAN HALWAEE.'

As we were pulling into Islamabad airport Tipsy said, 'Profanity is the sigh of the oppressed, giving laughter in a heartless world, like a rebellious poem, it strips the mighty of their mask of power.'